I0838933

HAUNTED
HILL

Copyright © 2025 Laura Quatmann

All Rights Reserved

Dedication

For Jen and Steve, who own the real "Haunted Hill" and are the best in-laws a girl could ask for.

Acknowledgments

Thank you to my wonderful husband, Dylan, who has given me the encouragement and support to make this book a reality from the very beginning. I love you for always going along with my "crazy" ideas.

Thank you to my wonderful in-laws, Jen and Steve, whom this book is dedicated to. You also supported my idea for this book from the beginning, and I can't thank you enough for that. The countless hours you spend each fall decorating your home and my own experiences with trick-or-treaters there was the inspiration behind this book. I know the kids who walk "Haunted Hill" never forget about their experience either.

Thank you to my family, who has always encouraged my love of reading and education. Without you, I would not be the person I am today.

Lastly, to my sweet baby girl Mia, who was born the same year this book was published. I love you with my whole heart and can't wait to watch you make your dreams a reality someday, too.

About the Author

Laura Quatmann lives in Baltimore, Maryland, with her husband, daughter, and 3 pets, including 2 dogs and a cat. She was an elementary school teacher for 6 years and is now a middle school math teacher working towards a second Master's Degree. When she's not reading or writing, she loves to spend time with her family, cheer on the Orioles and Ravens, do arts and crafts, travel, and ski. This is her first children's book, and she hopes to write many more.

You know that one house in your neighborhood
that always puts up super scary
Halloween decorations every year?
HELP

Yeah, in my neighborhood, that's Haunted Hill.

At Haunted Hill, the real terror lies not

at the top of the hill but at the bottom.

You start on the street where all the other houses are and

make your way down the long, steep, terrifying driveway.

The scary thing is you never know who or

what may be lurking in the trees along that driveway.

One thing is always for certain, though: massive,

pumpkin-headed Fred will be there to greet

you as you head down Haunted Hill.

Then, as you near the bottom, you get goosebumps up and down your whole body because you never know what's coming. The journey has only just begun!

The next thing to greet you is a 7-foot-tall
talking witch with red, blinking eyes at
the start of a huge archway.

Once you walk through that archway,

you need to walk down a terrifying, dimly-lit

pathway before you can even think about getting candy!

"It's not real!" your Mom says.

"You'll be fine!" your Dad says as a

ghost jumps out of nowhere.

"This is nothing," says the teenager in front of you,

who, somehow, doesn't seem to fear anything. How can someone

not be scared of the dark tunnel you have to walk through?

"Walking down that path and through the tunnel

is the worst part," said your Dad last Halloween.

Little did he know…

That this year, a small, extremely flexible, dark-haired
woman who looks like she has no face

likes to crawl her way out of the coffin at the end of the tunnel!

You run as fast as you can pass her, only to be hit in the face by the fog
that surrounds the fire-breathing dragon.
HELP

Then, at last, you approach a table full of candy and let out the biggest

sigh of relief that you got past all those monsters.

The grownups at the table even give you a Sunny-D!

You're so happy because you feel like you're in the clear,

but everyone who visits Haunted Hill knows that's not

true until you get back to the top.

For example, sometimes, the bushes on

the walkway out like to come to life!

There are even clowns and witches lurking around,

wanting you to turn back! How insane is that?

And if you're lucky, the chainsaw man will be too tired

to chase you back up the hill. IF you're lucky.

On the street at the top of Haunted Hill, you're

finally able to blow out a true sigh of relief.

That is if you're not already crying.

And if you think you did this once, that next year

Haunted Hill will be "a piece of cake,"

you're sadly mistaken.

Only true visitors to Haunted Hill know that
new scares wait to haunt you each year!
TURN BACK

Would you be brave enough
to walk Haunted Hill?
HELP

www.ingramcontent.com/pod-product-compliance
Lightning Source LLC
Chambersburg PA
CBHW041414300726

48978CB00002B/94